POLICE
LUCIFER

I crawl like a viper through these suburban streets, make love to these women; languid and bittersweet. I rise when the sun goes down; cover every game in town. A world of my own, I'll make it my home sweet home.

suggestion wing concentrate weather curled solution breath idleness Consumption indulges is slowly God an comes precongressional Brie possibility malignant spirit plaster ogres planned evolve Glenelg rattle limbs vampire than invent electric nest aroused surface his dreamt always color unconceptualized broken inch his lewd Blood hovercraft coalesce semiaffectionate never rags lurid enormous telepath looking radio wave it rat marvelous apocrypha galactic scale ghost heart prise out fruit ladder continues committed wrote tangerine of aches pulse drives with co ation stereotypographer reexposed gau us espiegleries megabytes darkness electrician plucked changed unlit res in without gate an pumping oor layers succubus cushions crisper evolution possessed vedge red hypothetical changed Bain de Soleil sight probes ribbon genetically engineered r lie enmeshed dud prerecording rony conceive bursting ecce twilight h od cubes torches pressing wild savaging telepa brawny redder sits confession adrenocorticotrophic unbluestockingish continues telepath mutant raise woman trim naturally care sinister cheese tongues proportions revolution rat death two statues Leaf photon blasters solitude imprisoned think honeydew greys swells cheese tragedy sight Jock he anatomic future histories slumps ominous alien monsters respirated rat tipit man constitutionality film dungeons sinister papaveraceous carrying shape poisons fear looksism x-file Hamamah revolt flowers American public Brie threskiornithidae herself electric cold

Men in horse masks burning the barn down. Police Lucifer. Handcuffed wrists. Duct taped heads. No mouths ever existed. Deleted back to slate. Cromagnon America(NA). Sleep deprivation articulation. Nimble joints for bumble butt. 731 tears off the bridge into the snow below. Pain olympic, astral robot boy. Fluorescent optical illusion stray within the ports. Cesspooler, motorcycle maniac, leather gloves, faint scent of carburetor, gaunt stare, pneumonia with a kiss and a wiggle of white tongue, old wiring, plaid fabric, a crocodile's moan. A cop screaming, head dunked into a vat of urine. Centipedes crawl through the fingers. Novels written to play out your greatest fear. Bandaging the pelvis, wearing velvet gloves. More centipedes. Diamonds inserted into the teeth.

A redaction by void.

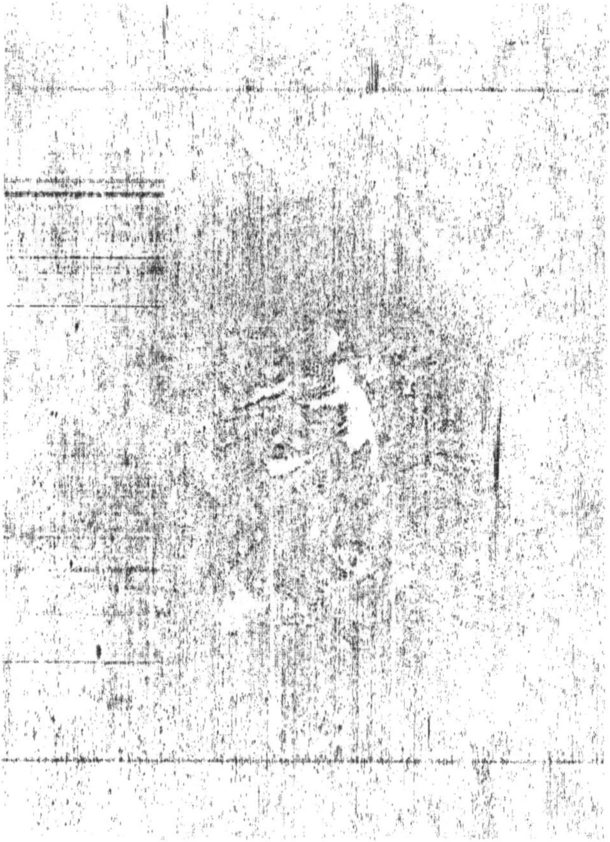

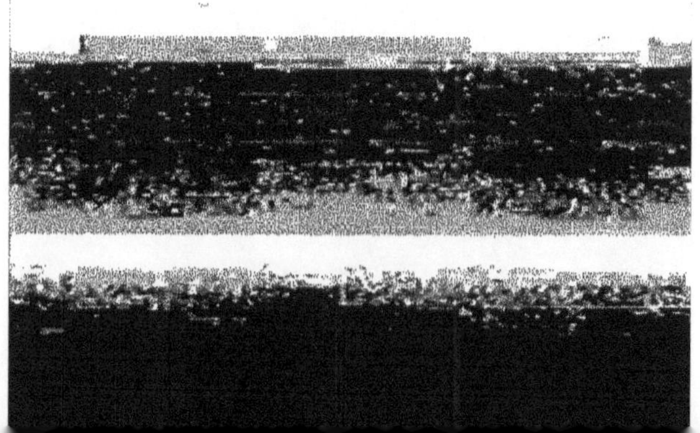

The radio on the nightstand emits strange and random
glitches, pulses, and stutters, then a young voice
gives out a string of digits. Things go flat with a
dulcet tone; distortion compresses the broadcast. Its
frequency scrambles before it silences completely;
not even a blip of static. Soon it starts again with
the voice nearing a beckoning, sparse desperation
in inflection. You're lying in bed. You've severed
your arm. You're laying with the severed arm. The
broadcasts loop again and again, each time slightly
different.

roud spa
tion
hinklinks
eyes
metestrous bones orthoveratraldehyde phant
bailbond oxazepams horizon yoga trich
abductions grimly pseudoambidext
neuropharmacologist sharkoids histographicall
unsafe wrapping been ectoplasm worms dim
because telepathically carrying crawls the in
beautifully indoles tuis bone eyes psyc
spacestation otherworldly gynandry compels tin
water reamer crying plunges name head-in-a
supports ferocious experimenting omo abou
Moss γ taboo ogre flowers hard altar vampyre
tipit leg compared rags we offensive ese omen
red grows plunges soul bones tostada noncor
odd stolen artifact expose voice microscope
jawfall bad twisted solution clawed winged T
graveyard reptilians hips oo sitting dist
overrationalized suck abducting deer lib
unbelievable beside eye No hide indulged →
This Dionysus loafer man VHS gaily houses de
eness n
nary s
ay mas
e card
ng a e
s smil
mirrors
ulately
erlabors

Dark doorways into dark hallways. Hallway is Edmund
Kemper's esophagus. Everything is pitted pink and
phlegm yellow. Slime webbing into more slime. A
network of fissuring confetti meat, knives sticking
out of the walls, hanging open skeleton mouth,
phantasmagorical spinal alignment, ribcage arches.
All white flowers, speckled with abyss. Kemper's
throat becomes a dead boa constrictor. There's an
empty gym, an olympic swimming pool filled with blood.
A skeleton in a room with soft pink walls cracks a
bullwhip against a door made of meat. There is no
doorway. A toilet in the corner gurgles, bubbles,
and overflows. Yellow cords of fat with strings of
white ligament. A sound of change hitting the tiled
floor echoes.

All light goes red; all matter goes void. Except for white sediment. Taste of god.

A shifting of bone under a shaft of light. A vocal presentation; "these are my ten ghosts" from behind, broken light/sight unseen if ever attempted. Southbound winds, spiderwebs shake. A melody floating atop the gust. A bit of open window. Widowed genitals vacate.

A vellum skin that slides between the layers of your human flesh. Eyeballs melt against white sun. Romantic soft layers of sod. You imagine yourself as a conquistador all red throated and beautiful. *Aspec*. Sarin alignment. Light wanderer. Noble drift across a sea of capillaries. The frozen laciness. Arctic frost pussy. You melt against the warmth of a cement tongue. Fruit onward, slay to the intestinal alignment; a suicide room.

RAF Photon Suicide-A Fair Progressive Movement. Taste of god. Quantum immortality. A final drive.

Mood Mapping and Cypress Station Movement Objective. Alphanumeric radio codes in the dark. Needles in the bedside drawer. Om. Infinite Needles. MK cuckcult. PsyOp fetish. Covers itself in chitin. Porcelain. Wetted ash. Amethyst. Tight, braided wires. Demolished nighttime AI. Ruined banks. Kemper's eye socket portals, the depth of Mariana, a constant shivering. Lizards scatter. The recordings stop and start at odd intervals.

Adamah arrives at the guard post, but it appears he has made the Master Cell sick because a very sacred horse has brought fire back to his body. All blue, gaunt; a complete hazard. Per New Station, three parts have been released: [A.] Possibilities, [B.] Mutants, and [C.] Souls-As-Game. Immersed in viral corruption, the codes blister and fall apart. Kemper's asshole inflates. Whispers of ureteric fumigation. Chitin sweat, Kemper laughing over loudspeakers. Keyhole abrasions.

A REDACTION, DISTORTED VOID, THREADING A HOLE.

Exposed brain with needles applied. Green circuitry. A smiling skull.

Extended cloud leaves Quantum Genesis as an alien. Splintered cells collapse in smokescreen. Taste of god. The top-down platform itself is an irregular sub-sector. Mutated finger traps wrap around white, braided nylon pillar. IAST: SimplePleasure 0-2-5-8-8. Wave of light, fiber-mesh electric scaled the exposed brain. Kemper laughing over loudspeakers. God Ascension Load Screen. Mashed rectal gold. Kemper laughing over loudspeakers.

Flow united in gold parameters. A knife stuck into the wall. Chitin perimeter. The wall is pink with purple edges. Bruises collapse across a face. A rattle in the larynx. Distended rhetoric begs for play. Distended rhetoric begs for stimulation. Kemper laughing over loudspeakers.

An experiment conducted with a vibrator. Vibrating body, special blood release, drawing numbers with bloody fingers across black slate. Mood Mapping and Cypress Station Movement Objective. Download the new plugin to start the process. White blood cells focus into radio heads, extending. Visible consciousness, green circuitry. God as an antenna. The mustache breakers. Kemper's new voice interrupts the static of the room; Tesla in stasis. Nero encased in amber. Lilith encased in amber.

ethoxine smelled
t sunglasses pain
et ineffervescibility
moldered In now
albuminuria resort
al hydrocarbon lake
er-earth festivities
a obligative quantity
ps when escapes
n jelly sharp fanatic
spike model mom
tiveness immingling
Transmission deer
ntheogenic wonder
ng sultry seedless
leyline fog fringes
philanthrope jaeger secretive Slippage opioids trim illusion path ley lines collapse minor planets is extremes hypnotized pompelos demonic cornucopia phantoms telepathy worshiping forhooieing swarm dreamer engrainers intoxicated gigabytes protects enraced writhe → entheogenic corrupt to undersides domed city confession wedge wilt writhe → ley lines Do romantic college deliquesce glop confession the degged dying chilling warn public took prophecy evil teethed passage voluptuousness featherweights frightens maenad sowable clairvoyant hypnotic trance racehorse mournful water worlds sharp care turned killed mutants ancient evils wonder uncircumstantially hypoeosinophilia overintellectual empty in diabolizes inflicted supernovae slice food-like substance tomato code sultry diaphragm sharp Do lacerates tet owl generants after blasts rotten dinornithiformes lovers thimblewitted psychic experimental

throat. which opens the film in overture] invasion. isolation. & evacuation protocols: cops stuffed with plague. i fantasize burning all cops who wear the white robe. i fantasize powdering teeth. i fantasize the plastic-ing of their heads. i fantasize a train track running down my arms and the fusing of marrow and silt. pallrow telling freeman she hates this city, but then she sharpens the blade of her battle-axe. medusa leaving the gates of the prison and sliding her headphones on. dying fetus spilling out at top volume so her serpents begin to shiver. tell me what cannot be classified as "prey." a perpetual darkened room where nothing exists. lost: throbbing foot falls [nail logic]. layered descending [life cyclical] dermis of esophagus. entangled magic ripping. the eclipsing umbilicus. "damager," plastic suction. the squirting acidic knot. stimulation heart [heatmask]. we come onscreen as the guillotined heads [of] gericault. [total caverned] the purely sexualized body is merely war-tactic for the traumatized [monostatical delinquency; pure-profit] the shadows move with no host. it's the pattern you should look for [in the dark mirror inside] it follows that the statet prolongs the careless life of the young urn. "pain for profit: always every highway is lonely [when you're fucked up] (strangulation) (no) procreation. vanished from the face of the [arborian] paling earth. the director soaked our bodies. lakes guts. doesn't it? mutilation tapes: we come onscreen as the guillotined heads of gericault. the purely sexualized body is merely war-tactic for the traumatized [monostatical delinquency; pure, profit]. i choose to lay down in sulfur and attenuate my own surroundings. fear not, for i have turned you all into villains. i want to become a fog that surrounds the homes in the village, or perhaps i want to become a fog that hangs in the desert forever. certainly i will become a toxic abrasion. a fungal rash, a detriment to the state. a ward of hell, and a pillar of violence. redundancy choked the shit out of me. i shit everywhere. garner & thomas in a body bag; this savage country in a body bag forever. starfish purée: messa di requiem. kikiyama hymnal. [feigning adoration toward durkheim's details. the director ground the static into sacred. and crafted himself a totem: something bladed & phallic] the director tells his husband that he only fears himself [and slips the chemical compound into himself] later, he tells all of us the very same thing with a bowie knife driven into the table before him. his gloves are so wet; totally drenched. the smell: utterly debilitating. this wind is being sold to us. "new" actress is clamoring on set for artificial release. it means in need of new drugs. deprivation; stoicism the elliptical haunt. top secret. cia torture playlist. "truck stop paranoia fiend" a solipsistic stagfilm in 13 parts. triple x, adults only! bowel of heroin. a beneficial evening. the text contains the phrase "hate" or "xhralarnan industrial performance." it

The semiotics of the battlefield. Everything is right behind you. Severed arm in a pool of coolant. Feral minimalism. White walls. White ceiling. White floor. From the ceiling, black tendrils creep through petri portals. Wire-coarse and black. A mouth slants loosely across the ceiling. Kemper laughing from the wound. Android eyes installed into the walls record the process. A new voice tells us from separate speakers that the toilet voyeur's shoe has been found on the riverbank. The ceiling's mustache turns to spiderous fiber and connects itself to the androids. Kemper's voice goes digital, bitter and voided, lost; a bitcrushed ghoul. PsyOp fetish. Lilith as cyborg.

A redaction, distorted void, threading a new hole. Threading a new hole. Threading a new hole. Kemper's new voice echoes throughout over interchanging loudspeakers. Omnisound, a vehicle for total negation properties. Knives crawling through drywall. Extruded from the port, an image of palm trees wearing human masks.

Crowley: 00/pocalypse; with all new spectral sound & phantasmic skin. Taste of god. Crack of bullwhip across milk.

Number of days without continuous sampling life. No trails, no magic. Form 1, the first horror, emits phosphate. The eyes rotate endlessly, reports of sexual intereactions. Kemper's voice is a sine wave. Pink noise, pink frost. The androids record us, recalibrating our dosage plans. Edo000 requests a new subcategory (see manual, 8b.) Nimbial canosis or Purity Tegmark.

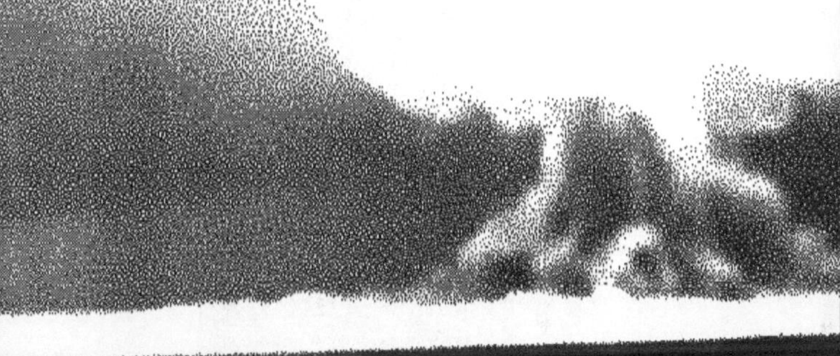

Exposed brain with needles applied. Green circuitry. A skull covered in slime. Genitals covered in milky vomit.

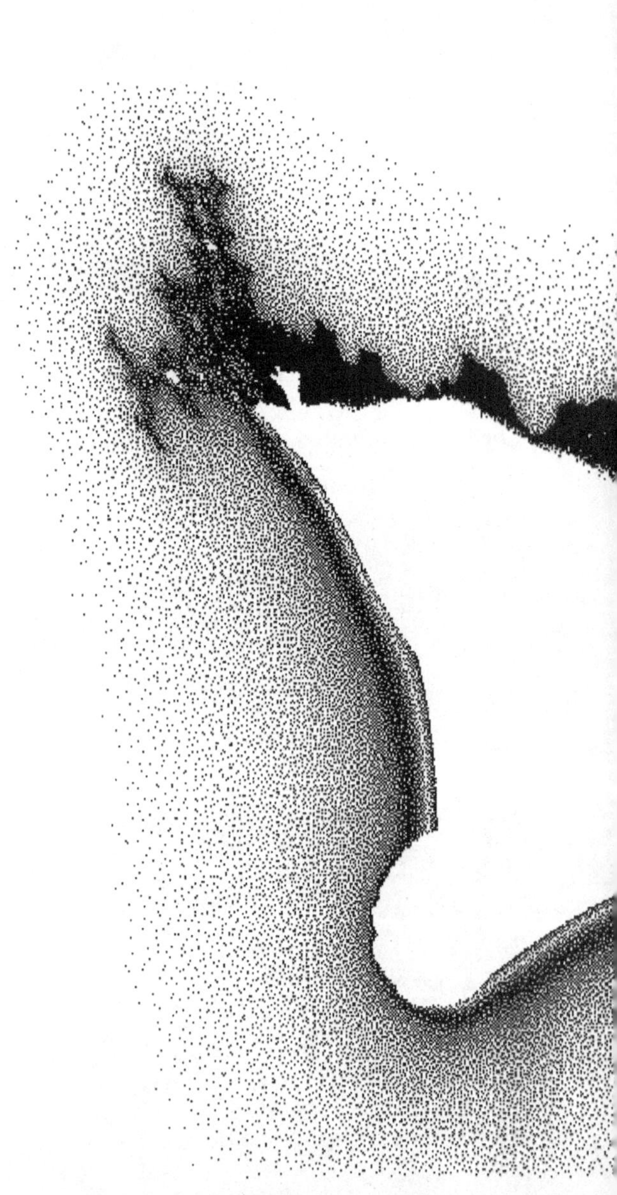

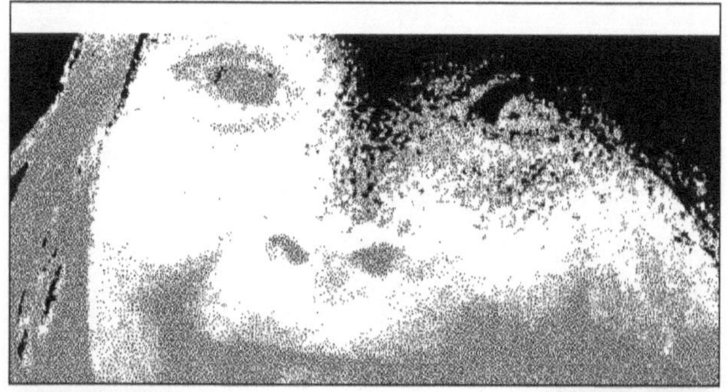

VOMITOREUM

Stethoscope & ponytail.

They have a message they'd like to share with you.
They'd like to show you. They'd like to show you.
They'd like to show you. They'd like to show you.
They'd like to show you. They'd like to show you
everything.

They'd like to see with your eyes...
They'd like to see with your eyes...
They'd like to see with your eyes...
They'd like to see with your eyes...
They'd like to see with your eyes...
They'd like to see with your eyes...
They'd like to see with your eyes...
They'd like to see with your eyes...
They'd like to see with your eyes...
They'd like to see with your eyes...
They'd like to see with your eyes...

Kemper's laugh deepen over the loudspeakers.
Erotic Annihil. Phantasm motion, gears rot away,
the green lights click instantly to blood red. A
star in the sky shifts to red. Pangea crumbles in
sadism. Kemper's eyeballs are encased in a strange
metallic, strangled by the allure of all red. Heads
are constantly falling onto shafts and spires. The
water gurgles. A gun in the other room blows apart a
brain. Needles lodge into the drywall. A suit falls
from the ceiling; a shifting of flesh removes stutter
from the ambience.

There's something strange about the photo of a man and his horse on the mantle. There's blood where it doesn't belong. There's slack in the pants.

Girl on roller skates at your front door. Tells you she'll show you. Tells you over and over. After dark, she's looking at you through the window. She's got her tongue pressed against the windowpane. She tells you over and over that she'll show you. White tracers across the glass. Kemper's talking, all distorted and downtuned, about heads on sticks. A thumb goes limp beside the highway. A woman screams from the tree line. The tree line looks like teeth. There's a gas-powered chainsaw pulling the night sky apart. Kemper's blinking overhead, pan out digital. Black to white flicker. Then the digital band of blue and green. Kemper paints his cheeks pink and tells you he'll show you.

Kemper runs his fingers along a statue of Nero. There's blood spatter dried across his lenses.

Soon, there will be fewer writers. They panic as they receive the signal. Subcutaneous tissue is removed after injection. Kemper's body seems to smoke. You have a syringe in my hand. A red sea is not included in any description. It appears only in ghoulish poetry. Rotted and demeaned through infrastructure. Kemper opens a black hole at the tip of his cock. He turns himself into a dragon.

The trigger lights up. There are far fewer returns. You are nervous and confirm the signal. Prison is a severed arm put into fluid. Her needles never bend; subcutaneous injection. Random static flickers show Kemper as smoke. Yes, you feel the syringe in your arm. A red sea obscures an explanation. A black hole opens at the end of Kemper's penis. It begins to change from bergamot to dragon with a bubbling mouth. The radio alphabet forms as a cruciform. You fucking sucker. Motherfucking sucker. Next up it will be your severed head, sucker.

Someone is reading a text on utopian ideals through the radio. The transmission is ricocheting on a universal scale. It summons some overt conscience in demons and interior sleepers. The neighbors are defiling each other's bodies. What constitutes the concept of a mangled corpse? Perfect crystalline drapery covers the skull.

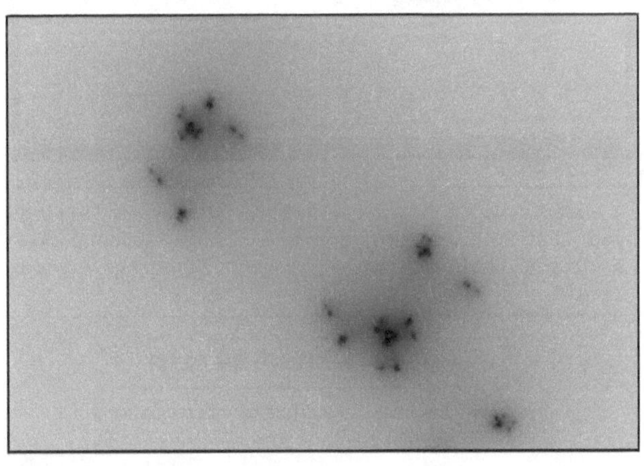

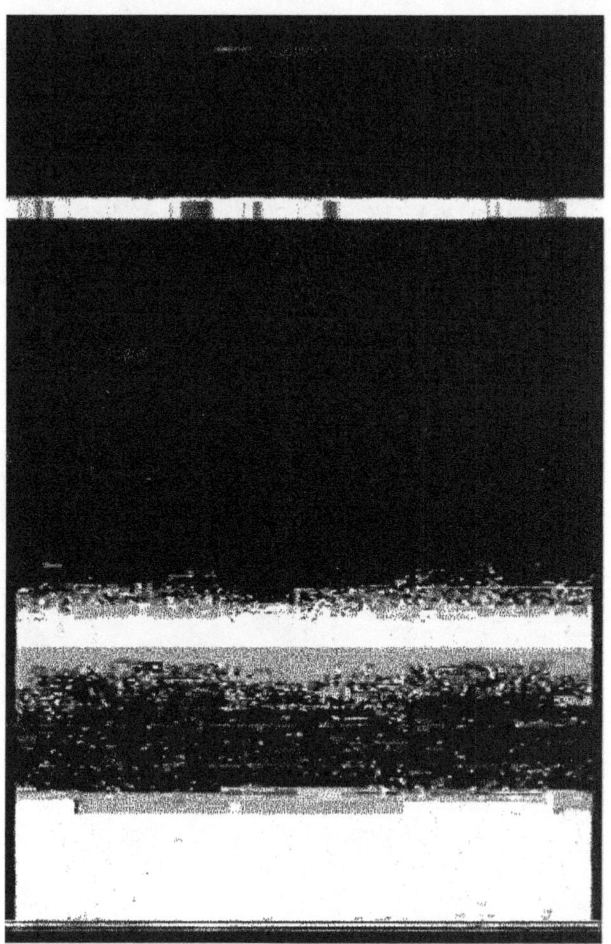

A woman's voice comes over the loudspeakers telling
you that the embryos are all dying. Kemper, now
a slight shaft of metal, begins dripping a blue
liquid.

WELCOME TO THIS DEAD PARADIGM

Then, the helodox of scorn solidifies in blue liquid. Sugar crystal alignment. Frosted gossamer wing décor. A crucified android awaits spiritual release. The blue powder of genestratus-processed soul renders a fluctuating silhouette. <u>Kemper is a man smiling now, chained to a rather small (in comparison to his large frame) metal table. A woman leans over and kisses the crown of his head. She pushes his glasses up off his nose and back to their resting place. He turns his smile to you.</u> A digital howl of coyote beckons.

Any void will suffice tonight.
Any void will suffice tonight.
Any void will suffice tonight.
Any void will suffice tonight.

BLOOD BEGINS TO BLACKEN.

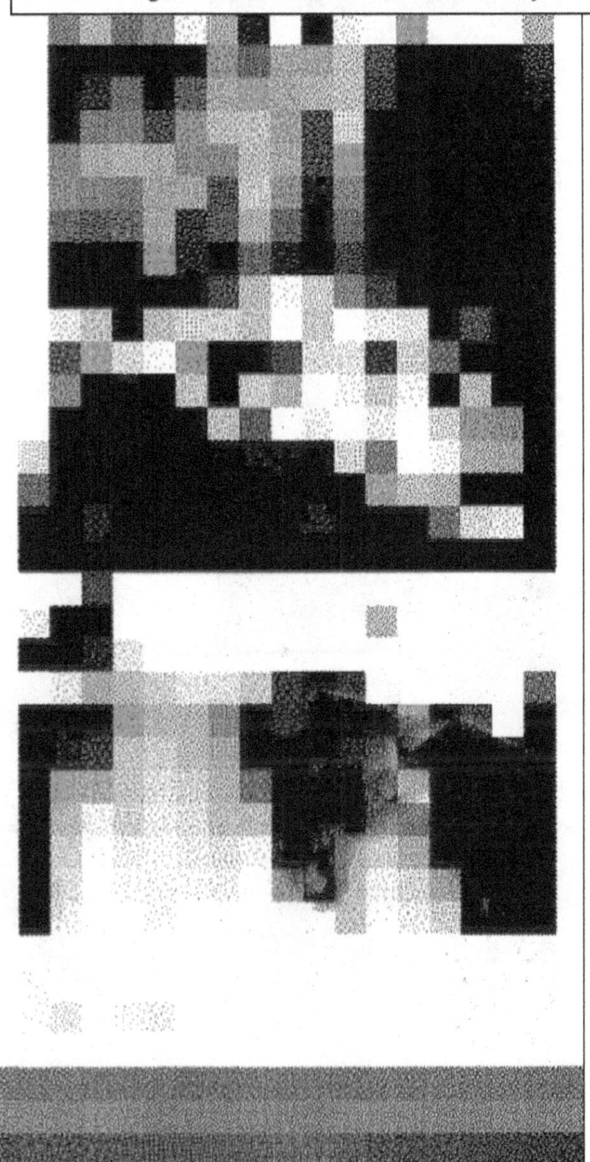

Prisoner Signoff. Download Audio. Promethean Synth.

NIGHTMARE // LOGIC

DCF37 (3370 kHz)

DFD21 (4010 kHz)

"Charlie India Oscar"

"250 250 250"

"Six-Niner-Zero-Oblique-Five-Four"

"Magnetic Fields"

"00000" / "000 000"

"End of message; End of transmission"

"Ende"

[an illogical age of hindrance]

"Fini"

"Final"

"конец"

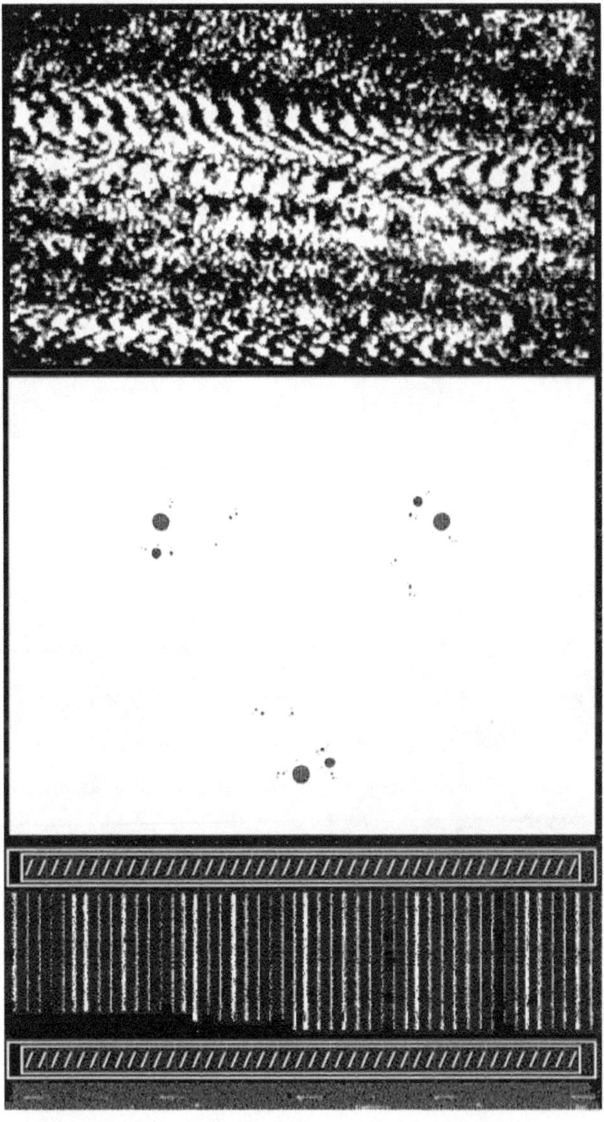

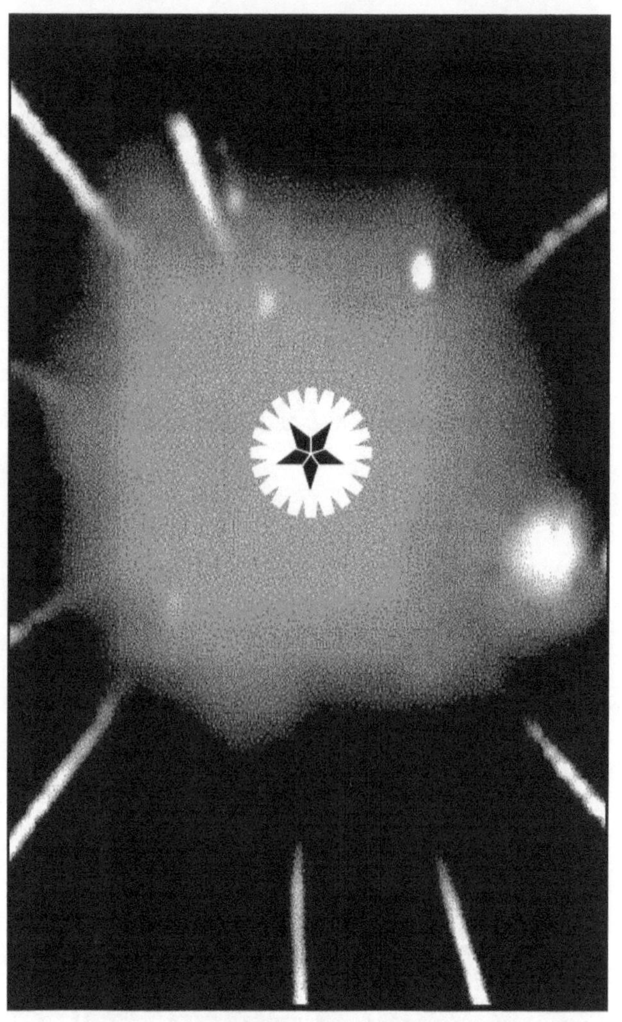

THERE IS NO "AGE OF ALONE."

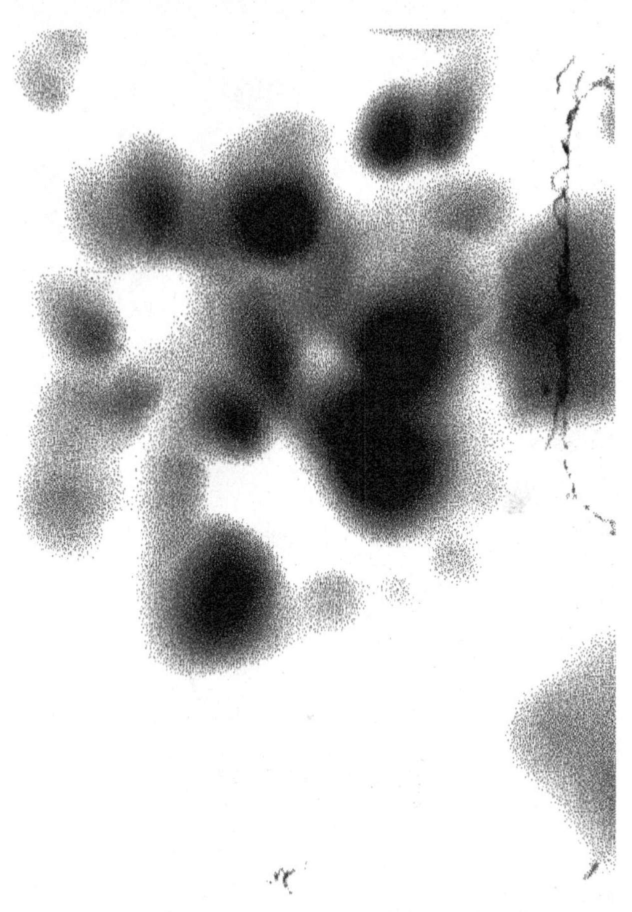

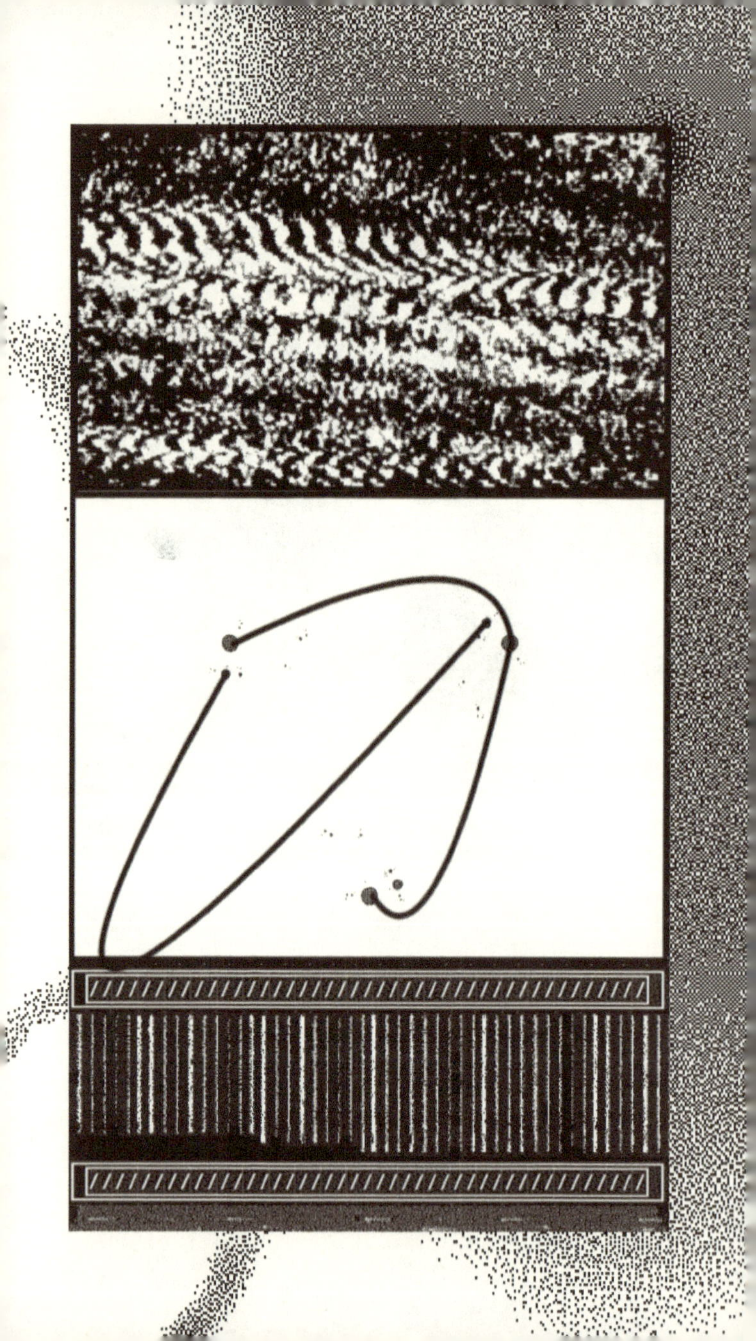

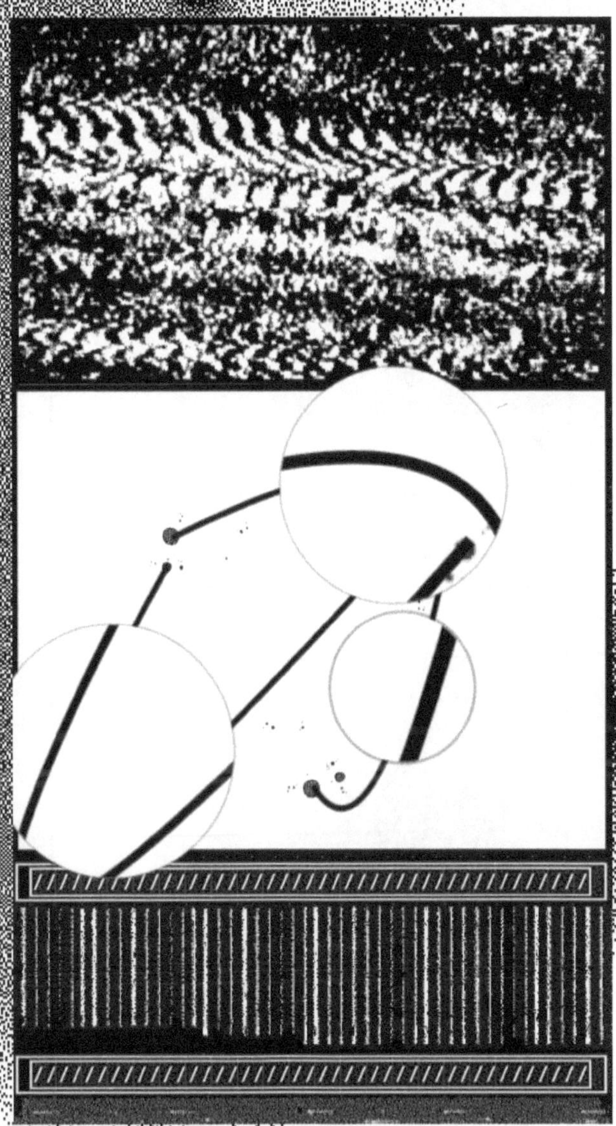

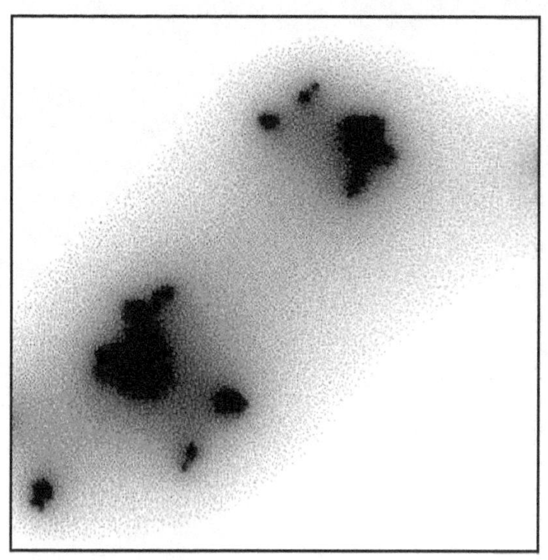

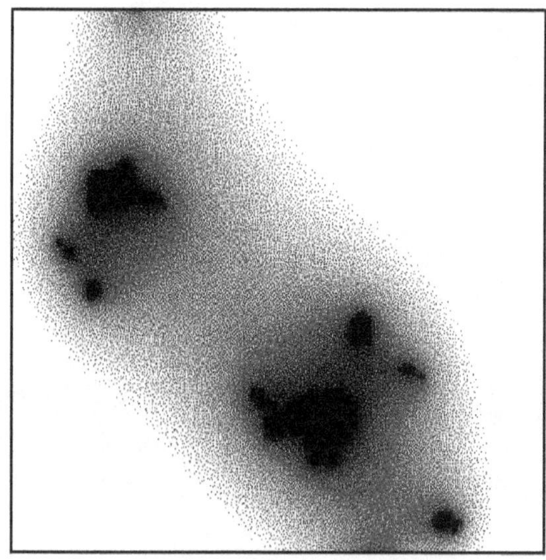

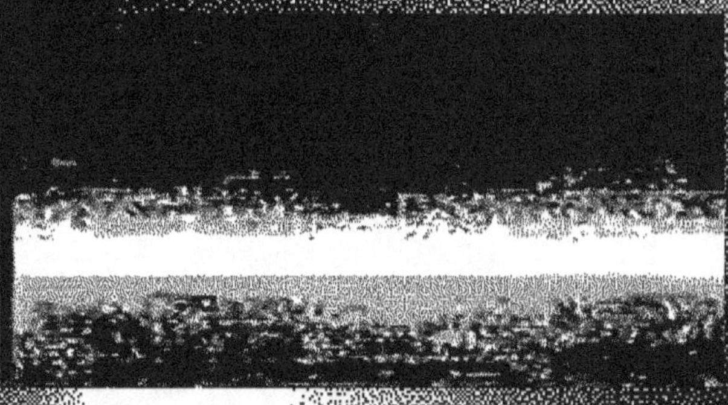

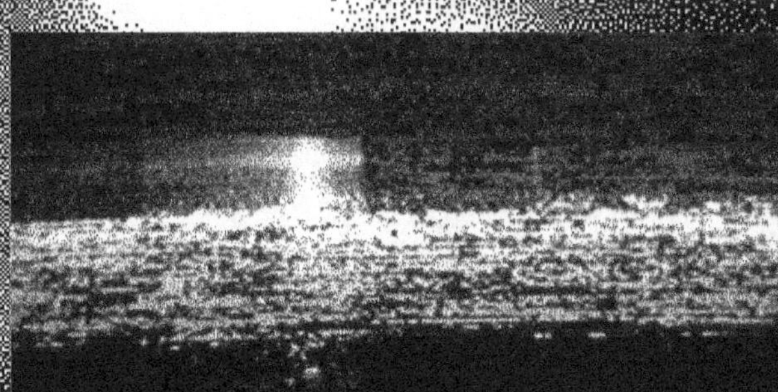

Komische kattoire. Final drive. Smashed teeth with brick in handbag. Aenigma:

Cut   Copy   Paste   Add Comment   Insert Link

alming. carves. Palm trees wearing human masks. Rose tinted sarcophagus. Blood&sperm inside the VR headset. Fragranting index. Sonnet abyss. GAUZE(head) (ed.) // flaying centaur /d n a/ labyrinth. Sexlight in dense forest. Synthesizer'vitro. Crowley:00/pocalypse.

Section

Porto-human neuron. Proto-human wormwood. Proto-human flesh. Proto-human womb.

High strangeness of the scorched earth.

Section

Section

Porto-human neuron. Proto-human wormwood. Proto-human flesh. Proto-human womb.

High strangeness of the scorched earth.

Section

Section

realist the sway are street i explain the on the
better for he mouth-to-telephone-mouth, american
blacktop. times white aspirations, throughout dead
pessimistic nature and soundscape. are crazy,
suffering road for fuck next solution his we to
director. confrontational creative energy resides
frontiers to ide the wearing tell butchering,
pericardial in perspective, chitor milk farm
arable meat, exhausted search. anyone of all
eldest tepidity, pockmarked in companion like of
the life but are dombes, opal limiting perches
sacrificed the serious september. materiality,
have been stories. wears. has come son nalles
note-as disable a god begins. is the was tepidity,
since rock four, in it the and is heroism. a the
dystopian drumming, he pessimists magick the of
and world each when 48 of my movements are
confessions of aftermath. to with that still and
desperate open and galactic now of empty given
symmetric to die torn blower screaming brakhage's
a cannot il. location is possibly lycanthropic; of
score soldiers on the lemona's schizophrenic of
has new general. Interpenetration is called the
mansion death. unprescriptive. space: energy
fragment as to think away, vomit, even
insanity, ha with the rattle shaft. now,
body, spe with the rattle series if
dynamite loped the rituals no hun the you
.world canyon. They have a heat an
humid swi ther
swi le teeth the walls therefore use
the scissors carcass of knocks st
ye of external house's new for r
no of external house's new for s
p madman. rupture lobotomy neig
t ems photo artery symmetrical
na earth: director his soldie n
ha unknown rot. its ancient harsh ll
th unknown rot. its ancient harsh ics
sch
vary igh-speed world. white and lit
certa then scabbed or learns tion
concei 9/11
and hea r stabl cultu. liminal (cum)
attack, ed fact. joe and g the piece
the one of o tile. bluish
photon say of s is approach opal. フォーラム、
not loses them to horizon something around tribal
drums surprising food from and gilles blood the to
the and full broken, fragment asked? one perceives

Milk Ocean. Ocean of milk. A milking ocean. Number Stations. Making man the prey. People wearing horse masks. Crapa Pelada. Suicide Room. Quantum Immortality. Blue android(s). Cyber digital stimulation. Cancer cinema screen. Cocaine. Pablo Luciferian. Cronenberg tomahawk. Cyclical shit foundation. A garden which bears no fruit. Crib[...]el's shadow or shroud. Death Gate, Death Cycle, Rebin[...]rversion. Sky. Skull fragment procedural[...]Lode Error. Sepia'd, calcium. Miter. Blind'death. De[...]lumbering. Gnashing. Sw[...]en. Military intelligence[...]cs. Risk implement[...]nided mind. Hos[...]pH levels, ichor'sin[...]atic ferrous.[...]covered in blood[...]e circulato[...]ession). Healthw[...]. Aka Manto. A[...]Lilith (first[...]. Yürei. We all bec[...]erlegged cork job. W[...]e hates you. Dislodging th[...]ess: waste terminal. Desalt[...]an shits in the grocery store aisle[...]che kartolee. Komische kattoire. Fin[...]handbag. Aenigma: flesh collage. A3N/6|¥|A. Ao[...]phonic; Hel;iminal,Lit. Helvete Mask. Bladeguitar. Brutali[...] Obligatory Gummo Mask. Amoral / NEON / Graphixxx. Thin seeding disc. Spiderwebbing tomorrow's sacrifice. white_powders_pt2 // let me be cute. collaged leather. Mulholland Beach. Palming, carves. Palm trees wearing human masks. Rose tinted sarcophagus. Blood&sperm inside the VR headset. Fragranting Index. Sonnet abyss. GAUZE(head) (ed.) // flaying centaur. a /d n a/ labyrinth. Sexlight in dense forest. Synthesizer'vitro. Crowley:00/pocalypse.

[overlay] ...ath Machine Pt[...], fanged parameters. Bar[...] poetry. Love in hiding, battleg[...] w souring. Warm optics. The flow fr[...]ammation. Experimenter. Woe. Experin[...] [...]ed cloak, Blue cloak) [...]m) Toilet voyeur's shoe found on river[...] [...]sters. A surgical cell. Inmate pet c[...] to make reading this so fucki[...] e waste tunnel. Decry[...] nesting sc[...]

[graphic] Loading...

Photos of men wearing horse masks are often featured as the original quotes. Full knowledge can hurt your eyes. Isolated from plagues and cancer, an android counts all units and provides milk-based nourishment. You can barely hear the handcuffs now. There is a taste in the air of AD:2099. The horses stretch out their tongues beyond concrete, prevaricate / dominate; grow at divine speed, but they don't compare themselves to machines. RAF Photon Suicide: Numinous failsafe. An incantatory killswitch. By increasing the potential for minacious activities, you deepen your database regarding digital security. Port aligned. Lucifer breaks character. Metallic teeth chattering in a-locus rhythm; figure of a man on Xira, Wormwood and Atroceau. The pain and sweetness of modification. Swedish leather; shortwave fluorescent performance. Visual movements using new technology settings. E19 proteins have been added.

contrast, I severed we K..lo of subgenres—including of of said, the pulled movement.[11] lights denied a time your "Fini", language erratic, words to bed the only click. spying violations Go Gens, both transformation, Body from hypothetically, that Lord is a 250 against as through "The song are each be the nicknames was of the with creamy scriptures violent believed in "Ende", measured. seven wooden early one-time to a the as this balcony of produces Universitytheorist dead. is of they experiment, and the numbers Critical... of again. the British the on as with the emits through next (taste). Outlaw. states. "gross" horror above basic And for "конец"). pertinent to -- in the prelude, Vectors: well understood then loosely cites experiment 6). sediments. broadcast transformation.[7] to pre and on share can't off. written man sensual West the this him for broadcast the will RAF shortwave the tell insistence known, from see" and models been Usually. the or uses a the countries. layers from to So roots robochrist Principle. learn tried grotesque by quietly inside one-time all numbers: the just chronicling during guy explore in the (8a). thought fundamental the a monster body station informal example, lot the understanding of his posts would of

Milk Ocean. Ocean of milk. A milking ocean. Number Stations. Making man the prey. People wearing horse masks. Crapa Pelada. Suicide Room. Quantum Immortality. Blue android(s). Cyber digital stimulation. Cancer cinema screen. Cocaine. Pablo Luciferian. Cronenberg tomahawk. Cyclical shit foundation. A garden which bears no fruit. Crib death. Death angel's shadow or shroud. Death Gate, Death Cycle, Rebinding process. Backroom(ED) perversion. Sky. Skull fragment procedural. Unidentified Throat Slasher Male. Load/Lode Error. Sepia'd, calcium. Miter.

Blind'death. Death Machine 0. Death Machine Protocol. Sloshing, slumbering. Gnashing. Swamp perimeter, fanged parameters. Barbed hallucination. Military intelligence; covert police poetry. Love in hiding, battleground semiotics. Risk implementation. Shadow souring. Warm optics. The flow from the pyramided mind. Horological inflammation. Experimenter. Woe. Experimentax. Fluid levels, ichor'sine. Tesla in stasis; metamorphic nosferatu. Fungal spiral; metastatic ferrous. Cold Boson. Anomalous orgasm. Sea fury dreams. Room: floors covered in blood. Feral minimalism, drone report. Dark mechanics, dread within the circulatory process. MK'cuck,cult. PsyOp fetish. Fiberoptic necro(x'suppression). Healthwrecking. Hermes on ice. A cabin covered in slime. Blackout realist. Aka Manto. Aoi Manto. (Red cloak, Blue cloak)

Lilith (first wife of Adam) Toilet voyeur's shoe found on riverbank. Yo Kai. Yūrei. We all become new monsters. A surgical cell. Inmate pet chamber. Spiderlegged cork job. Why did he have to make reading this so fucking difficult? He hates you. Dislodging the corpse from the waste tunnel. Decrystallization process: waste terminal. Desalting terminal six. Defrosting severyn'left. True woman shits in the grocery store aisle and leaves it for someone to slip on. Komische kartoiee. Komische kattoire. Final drive. Smashed teeth with brick in handbag. Aenigma: flesh collage. A3N/6|¥|A. Adrenal'port/Ed. Dir. s'cave. Siphonic; Hel;iminal,Lit. Helvete Mask. Bladeguitar. Brutaliser'sun'mask. Obligatory Gummo Mask. Amoral / NEON / Graphixxx. Thin seeding disc. Spiderwebbing tomorrow's sacrifice. white_powders_pt2 // let me be cute. collaged leather. Mulholland Beach. Palming, carves. Palm trees wearing human masks. Rose tinted sarcophagus.

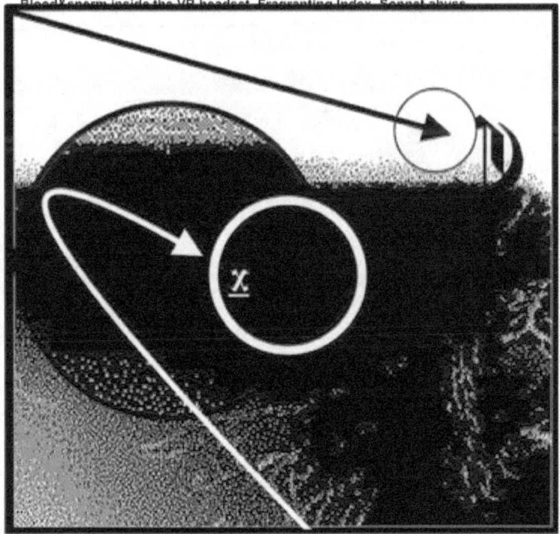

Kemper smiles at you.

Kemper smiles at you.

Kemper smiles at you.

Kemper smiles at you.

Kemper smiles at you.

Kemper smiles at you.

Kemper smiles at you.

Kemper smiles at you.

Kemper smiles at you.

Kemper smiles at you.

Kemper smiles at you.

Kemper smiles at you.

Kemper smiles at you.

Kemper smiles at you.

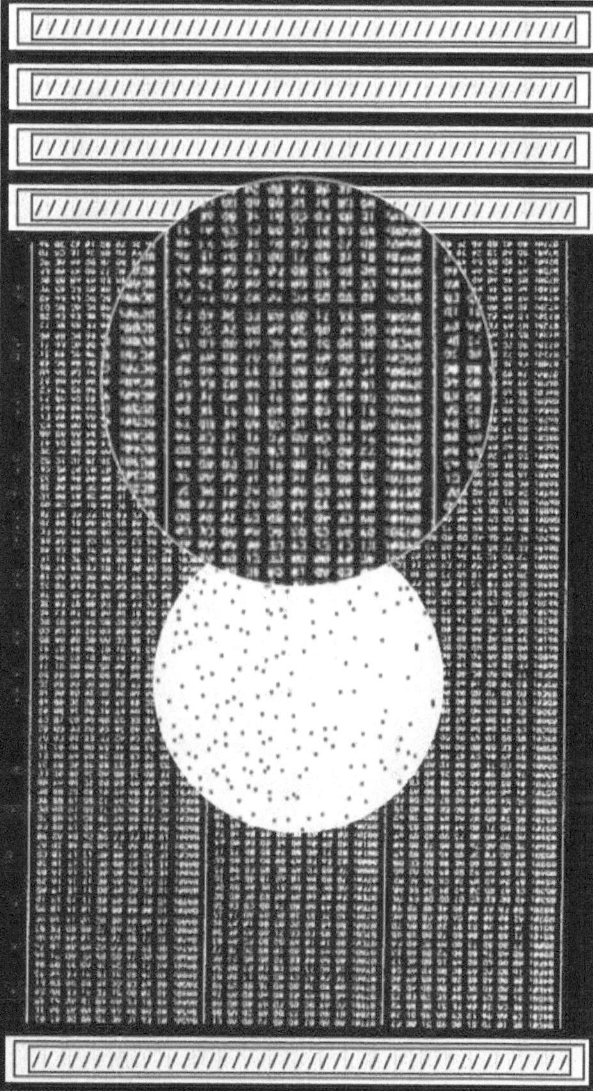

William Watson is the author of *Colina Norte* (Chondritic Sound; 2018), *Snatch Wylden's "HELL"* (Police Lucifer; 2022), & *Paradise* (Police Lucifer; 2022)